Hide and Seek

A Woolly Wombat Story

Hide and Seek

Text and Illustrations by
KERRY ARGENT

An Omnibus Book from Scholastic Australia

Sometimes I like to hide.

My friends look everywhere for me.

They look and look.

But I'm still hiding!

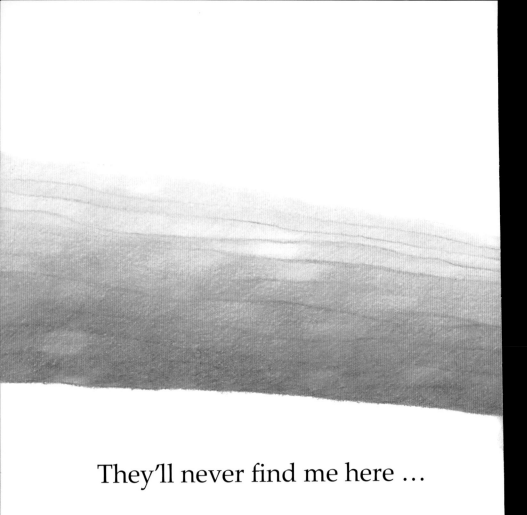

They'll never find me here …

or here!

Oh no!
I might miss out on some fun!

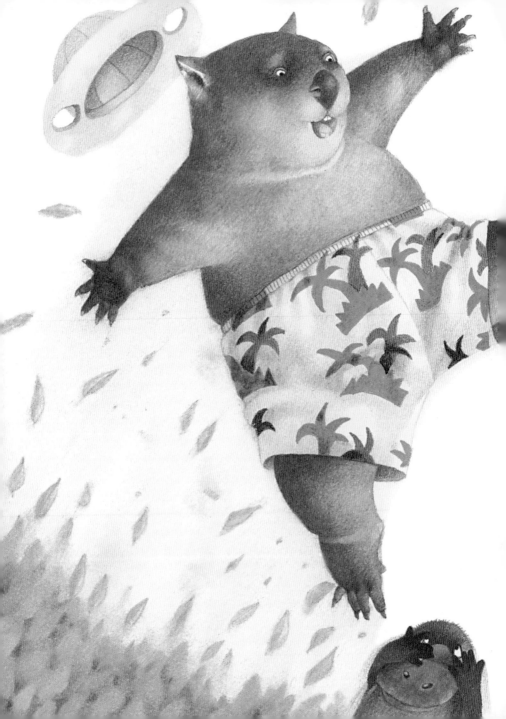

Surprise!

I like to hide …

but not all the time!

Omnibus Books
175–177 Young Street, Parkside SA 5063
an imprint of Scholastic Australia Pty Ltd (ABN 11 000 614 577)
PO Box 579, Gosford NSW 2250.
www.scholastic.com.au

Part of the Scholastic Group
Sydney • Auckland • New York • Toronto • London • Mexico City •
New Delhi • Hong Kong • Buenos Aires • Puerto Rico

First published in 1988.
First published in this edition in 2014.
Text and illustrations copyright © Kerry Argent, 1988.

National Library of Australia Cataloguing-in-Publication entry
Argent, Kerry.
Hide and seek.
ISBN 978 1 74299 049 1.
1. Title (series: Argent, Kerry, 1960 – . Woolly Wombat Stories).
A823.3

Kerry Argent used colour pencil and watercolour
for the illustrations in this book.
Typeset in Palatino.
Printed in China by RR Donnelley.

10 9 8 7 6 5 4 3 2 1   14 15 16 17 18 19 20/ 0

More Woolly Wombat Stories